IMAGINE THAT

Licensed exclusively to Imagine That Publishing Ltd
Tide Mill Way, Woodbridge, Suffolk, IP12 1AP, UK
www.imaginethat.com
Copyright © 2020 Imagine That Group Ltd
All rights reserved
0 2 4 6 8 9 7 5 3 1
Manufactured in China

Written by Corinne Mellor
Illustrated by Karen Sapp

ISBN 978-1-78958-599-5

A catalogue record for this book is available from the British Library

Bedtime on the Farm

Written by Corinne Mellor

Illustrated by Karen Sapp

It's getting late. Time for Farmer Jack to round up his animals and put them to bed!

Can you count them all as you turn the pages?

Farmer Jack stands by the gate,
He looks at the sky – it's getting quite late.
'Time to get everyone back home for bed,
Let's round them up and then get them all fed.'

SUNNYDALE FARM

'I need my dog's help', says old Farmer Jack.
'His name is Fred and he helps lead the pack.'
High up in the tree, two small kittens mew,
'Jump down,' says Jack, 'the line starts with you!'

Can you count one dog and two kittens on the grass?

They come to a field where Fred stops and pauses.
There eating the grass are three pretty horses.
'Come join us,' Jack says. 'Please get into line,
This journey back home could take us some time!'

Can you count three pretty horses in the field?

They all follow Jack; the kittens are mewing,
To a field full of flowers where four cows are chewing.
Fred looks at the cows and then starts to bark,
'We've got to go home – it's getting quite dark!'

Can you count four cows in the field?

They walk in a line along a small track,
Jack and Fred lead with the cows at the back.
Then up a small hill that's not very steep,
They collect Jack's five fluffy sheep.

Can you count five fluffy sheep on the hillside?

At the top of the hill, where the green grass gets thinner,
Six billy goats are all eating their dinner.
'Let's get you home and give you some hay,'
Says Jack to the goats as he leads the way.

Can you count six billy goats on the hill?

They all tread downhill as the light starts to dim,
To a river where ducks and fish like to swim.

Jack's seven ducks are splashing for fun,
'Come on, quacking ducks – it's time you must run!'

Can you count seven ducks
around the river?

They follow the river along a small path,
Where eight muddy pigs are having a bath.
Farmer Jack frowns before shaking his head,
'I'll clean you all up before going to bed!'

Can you count eight pigs on the muddy bank?

All of the animals come to a stop.
They've reached a hill with nine hens at the top.

'Come on, little hens, not far to go!'
Jack says as he spies the farmyard below.

Can you count nine hens
on the hill?

At last! The creatures arrive at the yard,
It's been a long walk, and they're very tired.
And although it's near the end of the day,
There are ten little mice still hard at play.

Can you count ten mice in the yard?

It's bedtime on the farm, so why don't you look,
And count all the animals that you met in this book?